THE ADVENTURES OF CHIEF AND SARGE PRESENT:

A DAY AT THE RACES:
A LESSON IN FRIENDSHIP

WRITTEN BY:
C.J. PETERSON

ILLUSTRATED BY:
DAVY JONES

A Day At The Races:
A Lesson In Friendship
(Adventures of Chief and Sarge, Book 2)

by C.J. Peterson
illustrated by Davy Jones

Published by

Texas Sisters Press, LLC
www.TexasSistersPress.com

©2021 C.J. Peterson

ISBN: 978-1-952041-56-3 (Hardcover)
ISBN: 978-1-952041-57-0 (Paperback)
ISBN: 978-1-952041-58-7 (Ebook)

This book is dedicated to my loving family, especially my biggest supporter - Super Hubby! Thank you!

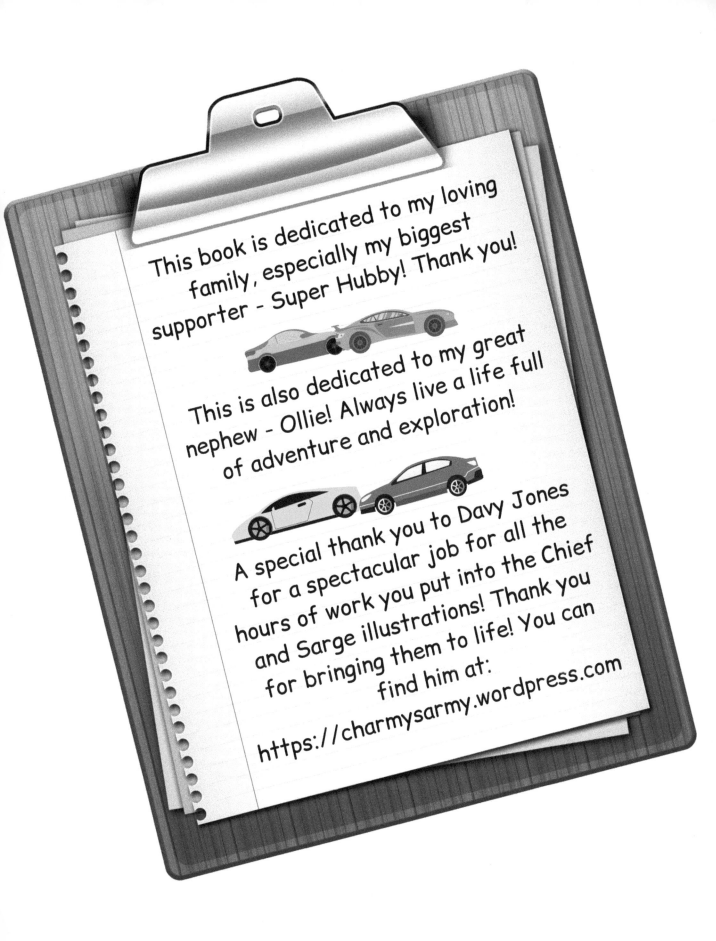

This is also dedicated to my great nephew - Ollie! Always live a life full of adventure and exploration!

A special thank you to Davy Jones for a spectacular job for all the hours of work you put into the Chief and Sarge illustrations! Thank you for bringing them to life! You can find him at:

https://charmysarmy.wordpress.com

"Today is going to be a busy day," said Trevor.

"This morning you guys are going to go stay at Sam's house, while Daddy and I go check out the street car races," explained Cassie.
Sarge grinned. "Racing? We like racing!"
"Why can't we go with you?" asked Chief.
"Yeah! We like fast cars!" said Sarge, as he jumped down from his chair.

He pretended to drive a racing car around the kitchen. When he stopped, he looked up at Trevor and pouted, "Why can't we go?"

"We want to make sure it is safe for you," Trevor said. "And if it is safe, we will come get you for the night races."
"Yea!" the pair shouted and jumped for joy.
"So, we need you both to play with Sam today," Cassie said. "You will be good, right?"

Both looked up at her with angelic eyes, and said, "Always!"

Trevor and Cassie dropped Chief and Sarge at Sam's house before leaving for the race track that morning.

When Trevor and Cassie pulled into the track, they were excited! There were race cars everywhere!

While Cassie and Trevor were at the races, Chief and Sarge were at Sam's house. Sam is Chief's friend. He and Chief are in school together in the same grade. Sarge sat in the yard, playing with

cars. He pretended he was at the races with Trevor and Cassie.

Chief and Sam played in Sam's playhouse, coloring and playing games.

"Where is Sarge?" Sam asked.
"I don't know. Let's go find him, so he can play with us too," Chief said.

Finding Sarge in the front yard, Chief asked, "Why are you alone out here? Why don't you come play in the treehouse with us?"

"Because Sam is your friend," Sarge said. "I will just wait here for Mommy and Daddy to come get us later."

"Sam can be your friend too," Chief said.

"Yeah," Sam said. "I can be friends with both of you. I like having you around. You are both fun!"

Sarge's face lit up in a smile. "Thank you!" Sarge said.

The three went up to the treehouse and played all day! Since they were having so much fun, Sam's mom brought their lunch outside to the treehouse.

Trevor and Cassie had such a fun day! They met some great people who became fast friends!

They sang the National Anthem before the first race it started.

Right after the song, there was a foot race for kids. They could get free money, t-shirts, and other fun items scattered down the track.

During the race trials, Trevor, Cassie, and their friends were right next to the starting line. There was a short wall separating them from the track. They could feel the loud rumble of the car engines through their bodies when the cars took off!

As the day progressed the summer heat made everyone uncomfortable. To cool down, Trevor, Cassie and their new friends poured ice on the ground, took off their shoes, and soaked their feet!

When the cars and drivers were not racing, Trevor, Cassie, and their new friends got to see the cars up close. They saw the engines, met the racers, and had lunch with their friends.

When they picked up Chief and Sarge from Sam's house, Trevor and Cassie told Chief and Sarge all about their time at the races. Chief and Sarge were super excited to see what fun the night would bring. "Will we get to meet the racers too?" Sarge asked. "I like fast cars and want to talk to the racers!"

"Definitely!" Trevor said. "You will be right at the starting line. When they are not racing, we will take you to meet the racers and see the cars."

"Will we be able to be with you?" Chief asked.

"Of course! You will be with us the whole time. You can meet and play with our friends as well! It will be fun!" Cassie said. "If you are really nice, I bet the racers may even sign your pass or your shirt!"

"Really?" Chief asked with a smile.

"Yes," Trevor said. "They signed ours. They even came over and talked to us in between races."

"Really? That's so cool!" Sarge said. "I can't wait!"

"Then, let's go," Cassie said. "Make sure to bring your backpacks in with you. It will be a long night."

From the moment they arrived, Chief and Sarge were a hit! Everyone wanted to meet them – from the racers, to Trevor and Cassie's new friends, to the people in the crowd. The happy little family went around to all of the cars and got autographs from the racers and plenty of pictures to remind them of their fun day.

All the racers got their pictures taken with Chief and Sarge! They had so much fun getting to know the racers. Cassie and Trevor got the little guys each a t-shirt, and the racers signed pictures for them.

Chief and Sarge really enjoyed meeting the racers and seeing the cars up close.

Back at their spot by the starting line with Trevor and Cassie's friends, everyone took photos before the races started again. Chief and Sarge enjoyed getting to know Trevor and Cassie's new friends. They soon became friends with Chief and Sarge, too!

It was a fun evening. They had a picnic of burgers and chips for dinner. Everyone talked about the upcoming races for that night. Chief and Sarge could not wait until the racing started. It was their first time to be at a real race! Sarge was especially excited!

When it comes to the Serenity Acres Crew, it is always safety first. Cassie and Trevor helped the Chief and Sarge put on their ear muffs to protect their hearing from loud sounds. Once the cars started racing, it would get very loud. Being right on the wall gave them the best seat in the house!

During the races, sometimes Chief and Sarge sat on the wall. When they sat on the wall, either Trevor or Cassie sat with them for safety. They liked sitting on the wall. The sound was super loud, and kind of tickled inside when the cars took off.

The races were short, but really fast! Cassie had Chief and Sarge wear the ear muffs, as well as a pair of glasses during race time. Trevor and Cassie wore them, too. That way the little family not only protected their ears, but also their eyes from getting dirt and rubber in them from the cars.

During one of the races, something scary happened. There was an accident! Chief and Sarge were afraid, but once Trevor and Cassie found out the driver was okay, they let Chief and Sarge know. Racing can be dangerous. That is why the drivers have safety rules.

As the track crew cleaned the track, making sure it was safe once again, some of the racers talked to those who were near the starting line. One of the racers talked with Trevor, Cassie, Chief, and Sarge.

When the track was clean and safe, the racers went back to racing. They raced to the final two cars. It was really late, but Chief and Sarge were too excited to sleep. They wanted to see who would win!

After the final race, they met the driver and told them they were happy he won. Then they said good-bye to their new friends. They were sad to say good-bye, but everyone promised to call each other.

When it was all over, the little family got in the car and rode home.
"Thank you for bringing us today!" Sarge said.
"Yes! We had fun!" Chief said.
"We had fun as well! I'm so glad you two could come along," Trevor said. "Now it's time to rest while we drive home."

Chief and Sarge fell asleep on the ride home. They dreamed of one day being a racer!

The next morning, Chief and Sarge slept in. After their breakfast, they ran to tell their friends about the race day!

Chief's friends were out of town, so he played with Sarge and his friends. They decided to go swimming in the pool.

After a while, Sarge talked to Chief away from the other boys.

"I want to play with my friends. Why don't you go see if you can play at Sam's house?"

"Sam is out with his mom today. Why can't I play with you guys here?" Chief asked, sad. "I have been playing all day with you. It is my house and pool too."

"I want some time with just my friends."

"They are also my friends," Chief said.

"Chief, everyone wants to play a game. There will be teams of two. There is no room for you. Go inside."

"You are being mean!" Chief said, and left.

Chief went inside. He got a book and read it on his bed.

Delilah could see he was sad, so she came and stayed with him. She could always tell when someone was sad, so she would go be with them until they felt better.

After a little while, Cassie came into the room. "Chief," she asked, standing at the doorway, "why aren't you outside playing with the others in the pool?"

Chief set his book down. "Sarge doesn't want me there."

"What do you mean?"

"He said they were his friends. He told me to call Sam, but Sam is gone today. Sarge said they wanted to play a game that only has four people. I make five."

"You shared Sam with him yesterday morning. And we shared our friends with both of you yesterday. Why won't he share his friends with you today?" Cassie asked.

Chief pouted. "I don't know."

"Okay. I am going to go talk to Sarge."

"I don't want him mad at me."

"He won't be. He is not being nice. I need to talk to him," Cassie said and left.

Cassie went outside to the pool. Sarge and his friends were playing and having a fun game of keep away. They were playing in teams of two.

"Sarge!" Cassie called. "Time to come in. Have your friends come over another day."

"Aw, Mom! Can't we play a little longer?" Sarge asked.

"No. You had a long day yesterday. Time to come in."

"I have to go," Sarge told his friends.

"See you tomorrow," Brett said, as he got out and got his towel.

"It was fun! I can't believe you got to meet all those racers yesterday!" Joe said, wrapped in his towel.

"Let's play again tomorrow!" Rick said. "We can play racing!"

"Yes," Sarge said, resting his towel over his arm, as he put the ball away. "Sounds like fun!"

Once Sarge changed into dry clothes, he went into the kitchen.

"Why did I have to come in so early?" Sarge asked.

"You like to help me cook, right?" Cassie asked.

"Yes!" Sarge grinned. "What are we cooking?"

"How about banana bread?" Cassie asked with a smile.

"I love banana bread! Can I really help you make it?"

"Yep!"

Sarge and Cassie mixed everything together. Then Cassie poured the batter into a couple of loaf pans, and put them into the oven. Since it had to bake for about an hour, Sarge and Cassie talked.

She and Sarge sat on the couch.
"So, your brother is in his room reading a book," Cassie said.
"He likes books."
"He likes to play, too," Cassie said.
Sarge looked up at Cassie. His heart beat fast. He knew he was in trouble. "We wanted to play a game, and there were only enough places for four. There would be too many with Chief."
"So, you sent him away?" Cassie asked.
"Yes."
"You told him they were your friends, and told him to call Sam."
"That way he would have someone to play with as well."
"He was playing with you and your friends, though."

While they were talking, Sampson came over and laid down on the top of the couch above them, listening.

"Yes. He was playing with us all day. I wanted time with just my friends," Sarge said.

"Did you not play with Chief's friend Sam yesterday?" asked Cassie.

"Yes."

"And, did you not play with our friends yesterday at the races?" Cassie asked.

"Yes."

"Did we ever send you away?"

"No, but you are grownups. You are not supposed to send kids away."

Cassie laughed. "This is true, but there is a reason I asked. We share our friends. We do not think they are only our friends. To us, they're anyone's friends who wants to be friends with them."

Sampson cleared his throat to get their attention.

"I cannot help but hear you talking," Sampson said.

"Sarge made Chief leave, so he and his friends could play a game for only four people," Cassie said. "Chief made five."

"Why did they not just play a game for five?" Sampson asked.

"Because we wanted to play a game for four!" Sarge said, crossing his arms.

Sampson tapped Sarge's head with his paw. When Sarge looked up at him, he said, "Let me share a story with you..."

"A few months ago, Mom and Dad brought you home," Sampson started. "At first, I was upset. It was bad enough I had to share Mom and Dad with Delilah. Now there were two more people I would have to share them with. That would take more time away from me."

Sarge looked up at him, sad.

"Over time," Sampson said, "I began to see how much fun you two were. I saw that Mom and Dad had plenty of time for all of us. They take trips with the two of you. Then when they get home, they spend a little extra time with me and Delilah. They have enough love for everyone. I also learned that I love you, Chief, and Delilah. No matter what you all play, you make sure to include me."

"You are family," Sarge said. "We always make time for –" Sarge stopped. He knew what Cassie and Sampson were trying to tell him. "I was mean to Chief," Sarge said. "I love him. I need to make room in my life for him and my friends."

"Actually, family comes first. Friends are great," Cassie said, "but family will always be there for you no matter what. Now, in a little bit, we are going to pull the banana bread from the oven."

"When we do, we can have some, right?" Sarge asked.

"Yes."

"Can I share some with Chief?" Sarge asked.

"I think that's a great idea!" Cassie said. "Sharing what we have – friends, food, and our stuff – with family is important."

"I get it," Sarge said. "I need to tell him I'm sorry."

"Now you get it," Cassie said, giving Sarge a hug, and a kiss on his head.

After the bread cooled, Sarge walked in with Sampson to take Chief some bread. Chief was still reading on his bed with Delilah beside him.

"Chief, Mommy and I made banana bread. Do you want some?" Sarge asked, giving him the bread.

"Thank you." Chief took the bread. "It smells good!"

As they ate, Sarge said, "I am sorry for making you leave. Mommy and Sampson talked to me about sharing...mainly about sharing my friends. Mommy said they share their friends with us all the time. Sampson talked about sharing Mommy and Daddy when we joined the family. Sampson said one of the ways we show love is by sharing. We always make time for family, because we love them. I don't think we should share our friends."

"What? Why not?" Chief asked.

"Because my friends are your friends. And your friends are my friends. We don't have to share, because our friends are people, not things. We can be friends with anyone."

"What about our stuff?"

"That's ours too. There are some things that are just yours or just mine. However, when we love each other, we share," Sarge said.

"I agree!" Chief said with a smile.

Later that night at dinner, Trevor went into the bedroom and brought something out in a bag. He handed it to Cassie. "I got something today while I was in town."

Taking the bag, she asked, "What is it?"

"Open it," Trevor said.

When Cassie opened the bag, she pulled out a picture in a frame. She smiled as she looked at the picture.

"What is it?" Chief asked.

"Yeah. It looks like it makes you happy," Sarge said.

"It's a picture of all of us yesterday at the races. It is everyone – us, all our friends, and you two," she said passing the picture to them. "I am happy, because it reminds me of our fun day, and all the great people we met!"

"I am glad you shared your day at the races and your new friends with us," Chief said.
"Of course!" Cassie said. "We love you! We always share with those we love!"

Until next time, you can enjoy The Real Life Adventures of Chief and Sarge online for some Family-friendly fun!

"Every Day Is An Adventure With These Two!"

https://cjpetersonwrites.com/chief-and-sarge

A Lesson In Friendship by Chief and Sarge

Sarge said, "I don't think we should share our friends."

"What? Why not?" Chief asked.

"Because my friends are your friends. And your friends are my friends. We don't have to share, because our friends are people, not things. We can be friends with anyone."

"What about our stuff?"

"That's ours too. There are some things that are just yours or just mine. However, when we love each other, we share," Sarge said.

About Chief and Sarge

Chief and Sarge are two adorable little guys who love adventure! Their biggest adventure was the day they were adopted by Trevor and Cassie from the Little Lamb Orphanage, deep in East Texas. Trevor is a retired Navy Senior Chief, who also worked with the Marines. So, when Trevor found them in the orphanage, and found out their names, he knew they were meant for them. He told Cassie about them, and the rest, so they say, is history!

When Trevor and Cassie took them home with them, Chief (the koala) and Sarge (the monkey) were pleasantly surprised to find that they were surrounded by lots of family. Trevor's service dog, Delilah, is an energetic and nurturing sweetheart, who looks after them as one of the pack. Also, there is the wise old cat named Sampson. Sampson is always good for guidance and direction. Together, they all live on peaceful Serenity Acres. While they are not related by blood, they are united by heart, love, and loyalty. They are truly a family in heart.

These little guys create an adventure everywhere they go! They are a fun, life-loving pair that will keep you smiling! You may find the family out on an adventure near you. They go on some real-life adventures, along with some adventures in the imagination! If you see them out and about, go ahead and ask for a picture. You may find yourself on one of their social media accounts.

To find the links, head over to their webpage:
https://cjpetersonwrites.com/chief-and-sarge

These are the adventures of Chief and Sarge, along with their loving family. Enjoy

Fun facts about street racing (for the older kids in the family):

1) No one really races for actual cars. Many Hollywood versions of the street racer is for the drivers to put up their own car as the prize for winning the race. The winner goes home with both cars, and the loser hitches a ride. It was the main idea of the street racing gang in the cheesy '80s car movie The Wraith and the storyline for the Speed Channel show Pinks. The reality is few, if any, drivers are willing to put their car on the line for a race. Most street races are simply for bragging rights. If anything's at stake, it's going to be cash.

2) Tire size matters. When racing for the NHRA or at the local drag strip, classes can be easily sorted out by assessing the cars. On the street, that's a lot harder to do, especially when you don't know what the other driver is hiding. One of the more easy-to-determine factors in figuring out a car's potential is the size of the tires. Street racers make a distinction between 'big tire' cars using large racing rubber and 'small tire' cars using more street-ready tires on their cars.

3) Negotiation. The racing show Pinks brought one of the more combative elements of street racing to television: the negotiations. When looking for an opponent, pairing cars isn't exactly an easy thing to sort out. Before a race, the participants will look over each other's cars and try assess the other car's capability while trying to downplay their own. This is part of the hustle of street racing: convincing your opponent of an easy win to bet big while hiding what you have. While deception by not telling is common, lying about what your car has like NOS or trans lock is frowned on.

4) "Dig Racing." For most of us, the image of drag racing is two cars lined up next to each other, revving their engines, smoking tires, and launching wheels up for the quarter mile. For the street racer, this is actually the most vulnerable style of racing, as it takes the most amount of setup. If police drive up to racers, they're in a bad position to get away. For those who do it, some will refer to it as 'dig' racing, as the cars dig in to launch forward.

5) "Lengths." During the negotiations, one of the racers might determine that his opponent has more car than he has on offer. While the engine is part of what's being tested, it ultimately is supposed to be down to the driver. To achieve fair pairing, the street racers come up with a handful of handicaps that'll even out the cars. One of those is 'lengths,' where the car determined to have less power on hand is placed ahead by a number of car lengths (the distance from axle to axle on a car) as a start. This, of course, isn't an exact science, and negotiating a favorable starting position is part of the challenge.

6) The NHRA was founded to stop street racing. In the 1950s, the manufacturing that had helped America during World War II was redirected towards cars and consumer products. Returning military members were able to buy new cars, while kids were able to buy cheap pre-war 'jalopies' and put the big new engines in them. The Hot Rod was born, and with it, the menace of the reckless youth. Wally Sparks recognized that this threatened the hot-rodding community and formed the National Hot Rod Association (NHRA) to encourage young hotrodders to take their need for speed to abandoned airfields and dry lake beds.

7) The NHRA threatened to pull licenses from TV street racers. The NHRA, since Wally Sparks' founding, has remained committed to the idea of taking people's need for speed and finding a responsible outlet despite its more visible role backing professional drag racing. It's taken that mission seriously even to this day. When the show Street Outlaws showed racers supposedly racing illegally on public roads with NHRA stickers on their cars and official permits, the NHRA responded by threatening to pull the licenses of the participants even though the races actually took place on closed roads.

8) Street racing dates back to at least 1903. As mentioned earlier, the legend is that racing dates back to the first two cars being on the road together, but officially, the first records of a street race date all the way back to 1903. Given the cars of the time, it was a long way from the wheel-standing, rubber-burning affairs of today's street race. The quarter mile that we associate with the drag race came about from runway lengths. Those first races were more point to point, roughly worked out by participants ahead of time often in scratch-built cars.

9) Street racing can have a toll. It wasn't just the leagues and concerned citizens that threatened the youth hot rod culture. Jalopies weren't safe, and racing on public roads endangers not only the racers, but also the people that aren't involved and are trying to use the roadways. Today, street racers try and have a code of conduct that keeps them away from the general public, but not everyone follows it, and it doesn't always work. While it's difficult to determine if fatalities stem specifically from street racing, or just reckless driving, it's estimated that close to 1% of reckless driving fatalities stem from street racing.

10) NOS. Every scene has its collection of slang and terminology. For engines, there are a lot of ways to get power, mostly by adjusting or increasing one of the three main elements of fuel, spark, or air. Drag racers are fond of mixing up the fuel part of that equation by using a blast of nitrous oxide (NOS). This highly volatile fuel can give the engine a big although brief boost of sudden power. This is delivered through a bottle hooked up to the fuel system triggered by a button or switch. Racers will refer to cars that have nitrous oxide or NOS as 'bottle' cars.

11) The Code. While not everyone that races is on board with Wally Sparks' NHRA or the newer organizations like Racers Against Street Racing from the SEMA network, they do recognize they have to protect their hobby from the public and vice versa. For the street racer, that means no daylight racing or racing in populated or busy areas. The code also extends to how they interact as well, like misrepresenting their car or lying about something under the hood when asked directly. Things like that can result in the person forfeiting the bet.

These, along with more racing facts were found:
https://www.hotcars.com/20-little-things-about-street-racing-thatll-surprise-most-people/

About The Author

C.J. Peterson is a seven-time award-winning author, published since 2012. She knows how to relate well to folks of all ages. Her heart shines through as an author, blogger, podcaster, publisher, speaker, cosplayer, and the farm life! She and her sister run **Texas Sisters Press, LLC**, while she and her husband run **Serenity Acres** farm.

She has multiple series, stand-alone, and has participated in multiple anthologies. Her series include: **Grace Restored Series**; **Holy Flame Trilogy**; **Divine Legacy Series**; and **Sands of Time Trilogy**. Her stand-alone books are: **Strength From Within & Christmas A.N.G.E.L.s**. The anthologies she has participated in include: **'Tis The Season, A Holiday Anthology: 2020 AND 2021 Seasons** (Both books); and **Beyond The Sea: Stories From The Underground**. You can find these all on her website.

C.J.'s children's book series is based on the real-life **Adventures of Chief and Sarge**! She and her husband take Chief (stuffed koala) & Sarge (stuffed monkey) on real-life adventures in order to share them with your little one! People have fallen in love with Chief & Sarge, as they follow along on these adventures on their social media & web page! Many have even taken advantage of photo opportunities with the little guys.

The Adventures of Chief & Sarge: Every day is an adventure with these two!

C.J. Peterson's Amazon Author Page:
https://amzn.to/3ik8vSY
C.J.'s Square Store:
https://cjpetersonwrites.square.site
C.J.'s website:
cjpetersonwrites.com

Chief & Sarge's Social Media:

Other Ventures:

@authoress_cj

"While the stories are fiction, the journey is real."

43

About The Illustrator

Davy Jones is the creator of the nationally syndicated comic strip **Charmy's Army** which follows the zany antics of a troop of army ants and a silly monkey. Ever since he was four years old, Davy dreamed of one day bringing his imagination to life and entertain readers with his cartooning skills. Davy serves as writer, illustrator, and publisher for his famed comic strip."

A Day at the Races - A Lesson in Friendship (Adventures of Chief and Sarge, Book 2) serves as Davy's first work as a freelance illustrator and character designer. To see more of Davy's work, check out his comic strip's website at **www.CharmysArmy.com**. This website includes a collection of blogs featuring a deeper dive into his weekly comic strip series. Read the blogs and discover what happens with his characters once the strip concludes. The comic strip may end, but the story continues in the blog posts.

www.CharmysArmy.com

Other Ventures:

Blog   @charmysarmy

Pinterest

YouTube

Linked in

CPSIA information can be obtained
at www.ICGtesting.com
Printed in the USA
BVHW090949141221
624014BV00007B/216

9 781952 041570